Magic Pony

4. Natty Saves the Day

"We're looking for two boys. One of them is wearing a green and black bike helmet. Seen them?"

"No," said Natty. "And if I had I wouldn't tell you!"

Smudger's eyes narrowed dangerously.

"You'll tell me because I ask," he said, dropping his bike on the ground and advancing. He stretched his hand out to grab the reins but before he could reach, Ned lifted his head and flared his nostrils. He snorted a warning and stamped a front foot so hard the ground trembled.

More stories about Natty and Ned, the Magic Pony!

Look out for:

Or you could join The Petsitters Club for animal adventure!

ELIZABETH LINDSAY

Magic Pony

4. Natty Saves the Day

Illustrated by John Eastwood

For Bridget

Scholastic Children's Books,
Commonwealth House, 1-19 New Oxford Street,
London WC1A 1NU, UK
a division of Scholastic Ltd
London ~ New York ~ Toronto ~ Sydney ~ Auckland

Published in the UK by Scholastic Ltd, 1998

Text copyright © Elizabeth Lindsay, 1998
Illustrations copyright © John Eastwood, 1998

ISBN 0 590 19710 X

Printed by Cox & Wyman Ltd, Reading, Berks.

2 4 6 8 10 9 7 5 3 1

Chapter 1

A Pony in the Bedroom

Natty smiled at Tabitha in an absent-minded sort of way, holding a white bristled brush at the ready. The tabby cat lay on the grass in a pool of sunshine, front paws stretched forward. She loved being groomed. Natty squinted into the light and pulled the brush along the cat's silky fur. Tabitha rolled on to her back, purring loudly. Keeping up gentle strokes, Natty let her thoughts drift indoors to the chestnut pony in the poster on her bedroom wall. It was not an ordinary poster. Ned – the pony in the picture – came to life, and was Natty's biggest secret.

Every morning when Natty woke up she looked to see if Ned was still there. If the poster was empty, the magic was working and an adventure was about to start. But Ned had remained in the poster for nearly a week, and when Natty woke up this morning he was still just a shiny, paper picture. She wished the magic could work every day and sighed a long sigh, wondering how many more days she would have to wait.

Her thoughts were interrupted by her brother Jamie and his friend Ben, skidding round the side of the house on their mountain bikes before squealing to a stop on the grass. Tabitha leapt to her feet and streaked to the garden fence, clawing her way up to perch out of reach.

"Jamie, did you have to?" Natty protested.

"I didn't do anything!" Jamie unclipped the chin strap of his new green and black bike helmet before pulling it off. Both boys looked extremely pleased with themselves.

"What have you been up to?" Natty asked.

"Nothing much. Beat Smudger Evans in a bike race, that's all. Bet my new helmet that I would win – so it's lucky I did."

"Pity Smudger doesn't agree," grinned Ben. "He says he was first – but you won by a wheel and a half, easy."

Jamie tossed the new bike helmet to his friend and shrugged. "Smudger always lies to get what he wants, and he wants my helmet."

Ben tried it on. "He's frothing mad with you for not handing it over."

"Be careful," said Natty, remembering how big Smudger was. "He might steal it."

"I'll keep out of his way until he cools off. Anyway, Natty, did you know that Penelope Potter is in the field, jumping Pebbles?"

Natty scrambled to her feet, surprised.

Before coming out to brush Tabitha she had lined up her three china ponies — Esmerelda, Prince and Percy — on her bedroom window-sill, to look out over Pebbles' field. Then, the dappled grey pony had been quietly grazing.

"But Penelope told me she wasn't riding today. She was going shopping with her mum."

"If you don't believe me go and look."

Although suspicious that this might be a tease, Natty didn't need telling twice. She loved anything to do with ponies, as Jamie well knew. Not that Penelope was particularly generous with Pebbles. She would let Natty muck out the stable and clean Pebbles' tack whenever she liked, but it was only on the rarest of occasions that she let Natty ride him.

Natty raced round the house, flung

herself out of the side gate and across the lane, to find Penelope riding round the field at a steady canter. Pebbles did look handsome, his grey mane flew and his tail streamed silver in the breeze. Natty clambered up the bottom two bars of the

gate and leaned over to watch.

Penelope had set out a proper show-jumping course. There was a staircase, a cross-pole double and a parallel, and between each of these a row of blue barrels, making six jumps in all.

Funny sort of shopping with your mum, thought Natty, wrinkling her nose. Pebbles flew over the staircase and cantered to a row of barrels. Natty knew he would clear everything by miles. He loved to jump and Penelope was a very good rider. Pebbles pricked his ears at the cross-pole double and cleared it easily, and the next row of barrels. In no time at all he was flying over the parallel, having jumped the whole course. Penelope turned in a circle and stopped for a breather.

"Oh, hello," she said, noticing Natty on the gate.

"You didn't go shopping after all," said Natty.

"It's been changed to tomorrow," replied Penelope. "So I'm jumping instead."

"Can I have a go?" The words were out before Natty could stop them. There was a pause while Penelope looked down her nose and made a decision.

"Yes, all right," she said, swinging herself out of the saddle and offering the

reins. "Take him round the showjumps."
It was a dare.

"Okay." And Natty took them.

It was obvious from Penelope's self-satisfied smirk that she expected Natty to fall flat on her face. But Natty's life had changed in a way Penelope knew nothing about. Since the day Natty had bought the pony poster from Cosby's Magic Emporium, whenever Ned came to life, whether he was a pony the same size as Pebbles or as tiny as Percy – the smallest of her three china ponies – he had been teaching Natty to ride.

"I suppose you'd better have my hat," said Penelope, pulling it off and handing it over.

"Thanks."

Natty put on the riding hat and did up the chin strap, ignoring the warning voice in her head which said *don't jump*. Instead, aching to ride again, she swung herself into the saddle. So Penelope expected her to fall off, did she? Well, she'd show her!

Natty took a deep breath and squeezed Pebbles with her legs. Being a willing pony it was all he needed, and they were soon trotting across the grass. Natty decided to take the same jumping route as Penelope. At least Pebbles would know what he was doing, even if she didn't. She sat up, gave him another squeeze and they were all too quickly cantering for the first row of barrels.

They were in the air when Natty caught
sight of Penelope's astonished face and
realized she had made a terrible mistake.
Yes, her riding had improved, but Penelope
would want to know why and how. It was
too late to stop and they cantered on
towards the staircase. As they passed the
gate Natty glimpsed a movement in her
bedroom window and
turned for a better look.
Behind the window-
pane, a proper-sized
chestnut pony shook
his head.

With Natty's attention suddenly elsewhere, there followed a moment of terrible confusion. Natty expected Pebbles to jump but the pony stopped dead to find out what she was looking at. Natty sailed over the staircase by herself, somersaulting spectacularly, to land on

the other side with a jarring bump. For a moment she lay winded, then rolled over to find Penelope looking up at her bedroom window too. Fortunately the full-sized chestnut pony had gone, and instead of three china ponies on the window-sill, she counted four, which was lucky.

"Well, you cleared it," Penelope said, unsympathetically hauling Natty up. "You really should look where you're going. What were you looking at, anyway?"

"Nothing," said Natty. "You might ask if I'm all right."

"Well are you?"

"I suppose so."

"In that case, I'll have my hat back." Penelope held out her hand. "I thought you'd fall off at the first jump. Have you been having lessons?"

"Beginner's luck," said Natty, hastily. "I learnt from watching you."

"Very lucky. I'm surprised you managed to stay on for so long. You haven't been riding Pebbles when I'm not here, have you?"

"Certainly not!"

"I can't think how else you've improved." Penelope did up her chin strap and fetched the dappled pony who was quietly cropping grass. "I'm going out for a ride. Open the gate, will you?"

Natty was overcome with regret at having given some of her secret away and quickly pulled back the bolt. Penelope rode into the lane, leaving Natty to pull the gate closed behind her.

"You could come with me, if you like," Penelope said. "Borrow Jamie's bike to keep up. I would lend you mine only I don't want it to get dirty."

"No, no, I can't," stuttered Natty. "There's something I've got to do."

"Please yourself," said Penelope. Then as an afterthought, "You've got a green patch on your jeans." She set off at a trot along the lane to Winchway Wood without so much as a backward look.

"I'll never be so stupid again," Natty promised herself, darting through the side gate. "Penelope must never ever find out about Ned."

And she raced round the side of the house, determined to get to her bedroom as fast as possible.

Chapter 2

Green Bottom

Natty saw Jamie's bike at the last minute. It lay spread on the grass in front of her and she put in a flying leap to clear it. On landing, her trainer slipped from under her and for the second time that day she landed on her bottom – Ouch! – and slid across the grass.

Jamie hurried out of the back door, his

friend Ben following.

"Watch my bike!" he said.

"What do you mean, watch your bike! Fancy leaving it in the middle of the lawn for people to trip over." Natty got up, stretching her leg. "That hurt."

Ben sidled round behind her. "You've got a green bottom," he grinned.

"What do you expect!" Natty noticed Ben's bike propped against the shed. She turned on her brother. "If you did what Ben did and put your bike out of the way, accidents wouldn't happen. I could have broken my leg."

"Conjure her invisible, Jamie," said Ben.

"Good idea."

Jamie pulled on his green and black helmet, then zapped well-practised magician's magic hands under Natty's nose and waggled them around her head. "Split splat vanish," he commanded.

"Get off!" Natty dodged for the back door.

"See, works every time!" said Jamie, and Ben laughed.

"You think you're a conjurer, Jamie? You don't know the first thing about magic, so there!" Natty yelled from the safety of the kitchen.

"Green bottom, green bottom, green bottom," chanted the boys, pulling faces.

"What's going on?" asked Mum, arriving from the living-room. "Oh, Natty! Look at the state of your jeans. They were clean on."

"I just fell over Jamie's bike," complained Natty. "It wasn't my fault. He left it in the middle of the lawn."

Nevertheless, she could see that falling over the bike had done her a good turn. Now she could explain her green bottom without having to say she fell off Pebbles – something she would rather keep to herself.

"That's enough, boys," said Mum. Still laughing, Jamie and Ben swung themselves aboard their bikes and pedalled off round the side of the house.

"So what are you going to do now, Natty?" Mum asked. "You could help me bake a cake."

"No, no, I've got something important to do in my bedroom." Mum gave her a questioning look. Natty usually jumped at the opportunity to do baking. "I have. Honest!"

"Well, if you're sure?"

Natty scooted for the hall. Everything was becoming more complicated by the minute.

By the time she arrived in her bedroom, even seeing the tiny Ned canter along the window-sill didn't alter the fact that so far the day was going badly. She'd given away part of her biggest secret to Penelope; she had nearly had a row with Jamie; and Mum was wondering what could possibly be more important than making a cake.

"Hello, Ned," she said. "Everything's going horribly wrong." And as if to prove it, she tripped over a book lying on the carpet, and fell across the duvet with a grunt. "See what I mean?"

In almost as much time as it takes to blink, Ned jumped from the window-sill and changed size. Natty found herself pulled upright in a gentle but firm manner by Ned's strong teeth holding her sweatshirt.

"So," said the pony, blowing on her cheek. "What's up?" He wobbled his lips against her hand. "There's no need to

look so miserable."

"I should never have ridden Pebbles," cried Natty. "I did it to show off and..." She didn't finish.

"And what?" asked Ned.

"Because I missed you. When you're in your poster and I can't talk to you and we don't go riding, I get lonely. I know I've got Mum and Dad and Jamie and Tabitha but it's not the same as a magic pony."

"Mmm," said Ned, giving it some thought. "You don't want to arouse people's suspicions by riding too well, that's true. But by falling off in the end you did what Penelope expected. Don't worry, she'll quickly forget. She's that sort of person. As for me, I come when I come and I go when I go. We both have to make the best of that. Magic is strange stuff."

"Then I fell over Jamie's bike and he and his friend Ben laughed at me. And Mum wanted me to help make a cake and now she's wondering why I didn't."

"What you need is a nice long ride in the woods. That will make things better," said Ned.

"Yes," cried Natty, flinging her arms around his neck and burying her face in his chestnut mane. "I'd love that more than anything."

"Then please make some tiny steps up to the window-sill. Can you do that?"

"Oh, yes," said Natty. She was sure she could.

"Then you'll need to open the window, get on my back, and I will make us both tiny. Then we'll climb the steps and jump down to the garden by way of the fig tree."

"How exciting," cried Natty, and squeezed behind Ned's hindquarters to rummage under the bed. She pulled out a tatty cardboard box.

"I can make steps with these," she said. "They're Lego from when I was little." And she tipped out a pile of red, yellow, green and blue plastic bricks and began sticking them together. Ned looked on with interest until they heard the sound of feet treading up the stairs. In a moment the big Ned was gone and the tiny Ned cantered under the bed. By the time Mum opened the door he had disappeared.

"Goodness," she said. "I thought you'd given up playing with Lego long ago."

"I have really, only I'm making steps for Esmerelda, Prince and Percy in case they want to come off the window-sill," said Natty, saying the first thing that came into her head.

"I see," said Mum, looking at the line of china ponies. "Well, I've come to tell you I've decided to make the cake later. Instead I'm going into the garden, in case you wonder where I am. There's some digging to do in the vegetable patch. So we can still make the cake together, if you like."

"I do like," said Natty. "Later."

Mum laughed. "Good luck with the steps. I hope Esmerelda, Prince and Percy are truly grateful." And the door closed behind her.

Natty's nimble fingers worked quickly. She was already planning how she would sticky-tape the top of the Lego stairs to her window-sill and wedge them in place with books at the sides. By the time Ned cantered out from under the bed, the steps were almost completed.

"How you doing?" he asked, in his tinkly-bell tiny voice.

"Nearly done it."

Once she'd heaved the books from her shelf, Natty's construction didn't take too long to finish. The miniature staircase was the perfect size for a tiny pony. She was fixing the last bit of sticky-tape in place when the big Ned leaned his muzzle on her shoulder.

"Open the window and get on," he said, standing tacked up and ready.

Laughing with excitement, Natty flung the window wide before squeezing between Ned and the wall.

"It's hard to get on in such a small bedroom."

Somehow she managed to put a foot in the stirrup and slide up the wall before swinging her leg over. The moment she touched the saddle there was rush of wind and the space around them was suddenly vast. Natty's jeans and sweatshirt were gone and in their place were her magic riding clothes – black velvet hard hat, jacket, jodhpurs and jodhpur boots, shirt and tie – which turned her into a person nobody recognized. Ned trotted across the carpet towards the Lego staircase. It stretched high above them.

"Now," said Ned. "Keep hold of the reins and get off. You're going to lead me up."

"But it's so high," gasped Natty. "There are sixty-eight steps. I counted."

"Then the sooner we start, the sooner we'll reach the top! But remember, don't let go of the reins otherwise you'll grow big and demolish the lot."

"Don't worry, I won't."

Natty slid to the ground and lifted the reins over Ned's head.

"Off you go," he said. "I'll follow right behind."

Keeping a tight hold, Natty started to climb. The stairs seemed to go up and up for ever and she didn't dare look down in case she felt dizzy and fell off. Sixty-eight steps later, she arrived at the window-sill so puffed that she didn't look where she was going and bumped right into Percy.

"Sorry." She apologized automatically, but, of course, Percy, being china, just stood there. She stepped round him and led the way to the window, peeping outside. When she was a big person it was a long way down; now she was tiny the ground was miles away.

"Are we really going to jump down there?"

"We certainly are," said Ned. "Get on."

Natty did as she was told, lifting the reins back over Ned's head, although her knees were wobbling so much she could hardly put her foot in the stirrup.

"Don't worry about a thing," said Ned, giving her a helping shove with his nose. But Natty was scared. She couldn't help it.

Ned stepped through the open window and the closer they came to the drop, the more frightened she became.

Chapter 3

Ride Like the Wind

Both Natty's hands grabbed handfuls of mane and she hung on.

"No, no, that won't do," said Ned. "Take hold of the reins and relax. You'll soon learn to balance."

With reluctance, Natty let go and took the reins as she was told. The moment she did so, Ned jumped. Natty gasped at the daring of it. When they landed on a fig leaf, instead of the great bump she expected, the sturdy green platform dipped and  rose, flexing gently. What a relief! Ned balanced himself as if on a springboard, and all the while Natty found herself nodding up and down like some kind of a jack-in-a-box. It was such a funny feeling it made her giggle.

Then they were in the air again and landing on the leaf below. Each leaf became a swaying step and Ned dropped from one to another all the way down the tree. When they landed on the grass it was with an unexpected thud which shot Natty halfway up Ned's neck. She pushed herself back in the saddle.

"Scary but fun?" asked Ned.

"Scary but fun," agreed Natty.

Thanks to Dad having cut it, the grass was short and springy. Ned stepped from one lush blade to the next with an easy stride.

"Are we going to stay small all the way on our ride?" Natty asked.

"Certainly not," said Ned. "Once we get on to the lane it'll be safe to grow big. Then we can really get going." He stepped on to the front path.

"But if we stay small how are we going to open the gate?" Natty asked, looking up to the latch which seemed as high as the sky.

"There's a way through at the bottom. Part of that plank's rotted. The gap's just big enough for us to squeeze through."

"Oh, yes!"

"Don't forget to duck."

Ned trotted briskly forwards. Natty was glad of the warning, for the gap was low and narrow. She pulled in her arms and crouched. Ned was about to go

through when a squeal of bike brakes in the lane halted him.

"Knock on the front door, Henry. See if they're inside."

"Hold tight," said Ned and charged for the flower-bed. He was just in time.

The gate swung open and a pair of feet clomped up the path. They heard a ratatatat on the front door.

"It's Smudger Evans!" whispered Natty, peering out from underneath a marigold. "That boy's Henry, one of his gang. Smudger's after Jamie's new bike helmet."

"Is he now?" said Ned.

"Smudger says Jamie owes it to him from losing a bike race. Only Jamie says he didn't lose, he won. But Smudger's like that. He tells lies. And now he's got his gang together."

There was no reply from the front door and Henry clomped back down the path.

Obviously Mum was digging in the vegetable plot and didn't hear.

"No one in, Smudger," Henry said, not bothering to shut the gate.

Natty could see Smudger's mean face and behind Smudger, leaning on their handlebars, the skinny twins, Nick and Stew.

"Probably in the woods. A good place to get after them. I want that helmet. Jamie Deakin owes it."

"That's right, Smudger," said Henry. "You tell him."

"I'm not telling him, Henry," sneered Smudger. "I'm taking it." Smudger stood on his pedals and set off down the lane. The skinny twins said nothing, just nodded knowingly and tagged after their leader.

"Yeah, that's right," said Henry, leaping on to his bike and hurrying to catch up.

"It's not fair!" said Natty. "That's four against two. Jamie and Ben don't stand a chance. We've got to warn them."

"We will," said Ned, trotting back on to the path and straight into a wild wind. It spun them big in a moment. Now

Natty was sitting higher than the gate and, as Ned walked forwards to the lane, she was able to lean over and pull it shut behind them.

Hot on the trail of Smudger and the gang, Ned set off at a brisk trot towards Winchway Wood. Natty kept in time with her best up down, up down rising trot, and wondered where they ought to look first for her brother and his friend.

Where the lane ended, Ned turned into the wood and the moment his feet touched earth he broke into a rhythmic canter. Across the path lay the log they had jumped once before. Now it held no terrors for Natty and, after Ned had cleared it, she urged him forward until they were galloping so fast that the wind whistled. They quickly reached the top of the slope where the path curled out of sight between the trees.

Here Ned slowed and they found themselves trotting into an overhung gully, edged with gnarled and twisted roots. Tyre marks snaked high in the bank's sandy soil.

"Jamie and Ben?" wondered Natty. "Or Smudger and his gang?"

"We'll go on," said Ned. From nowhere two bikers swerved across the path ahead. Ned half reared and Natty gasped. It was Smudger and Henry and behind them, skidding to cut off their retreat, came the skinny twins, Nick and Stew. Natty swallowed nervously.

"It's just a girl on a pony," said Henry.

"But there were two voices," said Smudger suspiciously.

"Clear the path, please," said Natty. "I need to get on."

"You seen anyone else about here?" Henry asked.

"No," said Natty. "Only those two." And she pointed at Nick and Stew.

"Not them, stupid," said Smudger. "We know them. We're looking for two other boys. One of them is wearing a green and black bike helmet. Seen them?"

"No," said Natty. "And if I had I wouldn't tell you!"

Smudger's eyes narrowed dangerously.

"You'll tell me because I ask," he said, dropping his bike on the ground and advancing. He stretched his hand out to grab the reins but before he could reach, Ned lifted his head and flared his nostrils. He snorted a warning and stamped a front foot so hard the ground trembled. Smudger backed off.

"You keep that nag under control," he said.

Ned didn't like being called a nag or the tone of Smudger's voice, and he let out an angry whinny, rearing up to slice the air with his front legs. Smudger dived for safety and Ned leapt towards Smudger's bike. Natty clung on, and Henry, fearing the worst, quickly pulled

his bike to one side then scrambled up the bank. But Ned didn't trample Smudger's bike; he jumped it and galloped out of the gully, raising a dust cloud behind him.

"That should give them something to think about," he said when they were out of hearing.

"It did," said Natty, aware of the four startled faces left behind and relieved she hadn't fallen off.

It wasn't until they were calmly cantering between the trees that she realized not one of the boys had recognized her – thanks to the wonderful riding clothes disguise.

Chapter 4

Ambush

Natty and Ned reached the highest point in the wood and took the opportunity to look about them. In one direction the trees sloped all the way down to the river. They glimpsed the path which weaved along the river bank, the water glinting in the sunlight, the far bank edged with trees and the grassy field beyond.

But there was no sign of Jamie or Ben. The only sound was a trilling blackbird. Even Smudger and his gang seemed to have been swallowed up by the trees. But they were there, lurking, Natty was sure of it, doing exactly what she and Ned were doing – searching for Jamie.

"Natty, think," said Ned. "Where do Jamie and Ben really like to go when they bike in the woods?"

"They ride the Ups and Downs, which is a track that goes round in a twisty loop and up and down a lot."

"I guessed it might," said Ned.

"Or they may have gone to the rope swing down by the river. But the Ups and Downs are nearest."

"We'll try there first then," said Ned. "Which way?"

"Along the ridge and then drop down.

The Ups and Downs are in a sort of valley."

Ned cantered along the ridge and Natty kept a cautious lookout. They met the path that sloped towards the Ups and Downs and Ned slowed to a walk. They listened out for tell-tale voices but

heard nothing until grunts of effort, the whirr of bicycle chains and the click of gears gave away that someone was biking down below.

Natty guided Ned between the trees to the top of a steep slope, where they took cover in the undergrowth.

"See, down there. There's the bendy path where the bikes go round."

Taking care not to be seen, they peeped into the valley. Smudger was the first biker they saw, pedalling slowly up a hillock and down again. The skinny twins followed and an unsteady Henry brought up the rear.

"They're still looking," said Ned. "They're not giving up, are they?"

"Doesn't look like it," replied Natty. "Do you think we should go down and look too?"

"Just to make sure," said Ned.

Turning away from the steep slope ahead, they made their way into the valley by the path. Natty didn't feel so frightened about meeting Smudger now, but, given a choice, she would rather not.

It was obvious when they reached the Ups and Downs. Tyres had worn the path wide and smooth, fraying any protruding tree roots. Keeping a sharp lookout, they climbed and twisted and turned around the looping track. But by the time they arrived back where they started from, they had seen no one.

"Vanished," said Natty. "Not even a glimpse of Smudger and the gang."

"We've missed them all somehow," said Ned. "Better check the rope swing."

"Yes," said Natty, really anxious now.

"We've wasted ages looking when they've already gone. Smudger's got a start on us now."

Ned swung round and set off, back up the valley slope to the higher part of the wood. Cantering along the ridge, Natty turned him, searching for the path that led down to the river. Look for it as she might, she couldn't find it.

"I'm lost," she admitted at last. Ned skidded to a stop. Unconcerned voices drifted up between the trees. Shouts and laughter and friendly banter. "It's Jamie and Ben."

"Yes," said Ned. "And making enough noise to guide Smudger right to them."

"Quick," said Natty. "We've got to get there first."

"The voices are straight ahead," said Ned. "The river must be down this way."

"I'm not sure," said Natty. "I think we need to double back a bit to find the path."

"We haven't time to double back. Smudger and the others could be there by now."

Ned cantered straight towards the voices, although they could see neither the river nor the great oak tree with its swinging rope. He was forced to slow when they found themselves funnelled into a path between sharp brambles which twisted and turned and took them up not down.

"This is no good," said Ned, unable to turn back because the path was so narrow. Then unexpectedly, they emerged on to a rocky plateau. "Where are we now?"

"This is where Mum and Dad come blackberrying," said Natty, realizing the horrible truth of it. "We're on the cliff. We can't get down to the river from here. It's a bramble-covered precipice. We've got to go back."

Looking below, her eye caught something swinging between the trees. Ned stepped a little nearer to the edge and they looked down over the brambles. They could see the river and Jamie, swinging out across the water on a rope.

"Now what do we do?" asked Natty. Ben sat on a tree root, his feet idly dangling in the flow. "This is hopeless." The boys' bikes leaned against the far side of the broad oak, and, hanging from one of the saddles, was Jamie's new green and black bike helmet. "The helmet! Why isn't he wearing it?" Natty groaned. "Why's he swinging when he should be keeping a lookout?"

"Because he doesn't know that Smudger and his friends are after him," said Ned, grimly.

The words were no sooner said than Smudger and the gang arrived, not on their bikes but creeping close to the ground, out of sight. It was Henry who spotted the helmet. He gave a wave and pointed. Smudger signalled to the others to retreat and stood up.

Natty could contain herself no longer and, rising in the stirrups, took a deep breath.

"Jamie!" she yelled. "Watch out!"

Startled pigeons burst between the branches and a jay shrieked a warning. Swinging out across the water, Jamie turned in time to see Smudger snatch the green and black helmet and run.

"Quick, Ben, grab him!"

But Ben scrambled up the bank too

late. By the time he reached the bikes, Smudger had the helmet on his head and was leaping astride his own machine, which Stew held ready for him. With victorious whoops, the four boys pedalled off leaving Jamie to jump to the bank and angrily kick a tree root. Natty slumped back into the saddle in despair.

"Now what do we do?" she asked.

Chapter 5

Splash! Splash!

Ned reared up and spun round, almost landing Natty in a bramble bush. Somehow she stayed on.

"We cut them off," he said. "That's what we do. Hold tight."

Natty grabbed a handful of mane as Ned twisted and turned along the narrow bramble path and galloped back between the trees, slithering down towards the river path to cut off the gang's escape. Natty saw the boys glide between the trees, laughing, shouting, victorious, with the green and black bike helmet fastened on Smudger's head.

Ned cantered on to the path, ears flat back, and galloped straight towards them.

Smudger was the first to see him and spun to a startled halt. The twins stopped behind him but Henry had to swerve and ended up in a heap.

"Back," shouted Smudger. "Back the other way. It's that girl on that maniac pony."

The boys turned and retreated fast the way they had come. Henry struggled to his feet and, with an alarmed look over his shoulder, raced to get away.

"We've got to stop them. They could escape across the bridge," said Natty. "It takes you over the river to the field."

"Where is the bridge?" Ned asked.

"It's where the path bends. A wooden platform sort of bridge. Just there!"

No sooner had Natty explained than the bridge came into view and cantering towards it across the field was Penelope Potter on Pebbles. Jamie and Ben, pedalling furiously, had almost reached it too, and shouted gleefully when they saw Smudger had changed direction and was heading back towards them. Even though Smudger was going his fastest to get there first, it seemed to Natty that everyone was going to arrive at the bridge at the same time.

Penelope and Pebbles had just started across when Smudger turned his bike on to the planks. Jamie and Ben were almost upon him and he was desperate to lead his gang to safety. But the bridge was too narrow for a bike and pony to pass one another.

"Get out of the way," yelled Smudger. "I got to get over!"

"Don't be stupid," shouted Penelope. "Give way to horses." And as Smudger tried to push past she took her foot from the stirrup and gave him a shove.

Smudger completely lost his balance, and bike and boy toppled into the water with a mighty splash. Unfortunately for Penelope, the splash so startled Pebbles that he half reared and jumped between the remaining gang members for the bank. Penelope also lost her balance and with a cry of dismay toppled over the other side of the bridge.

Another splash was too much for Pebbles. Seeing the path for home he bolted down it and came galloping towards Natty and Ned, reins and stirrups flying. Natty just had time to see Jamie jump in to help Penelope before Ned whinnied and turned to keep pace with the frightened Pebbles.

"Take hold of his reins, Natty," Ned said. Natty stretched out to grab them – not so easy when going at speed and trying to keep your balance. It seemed an age before she managed to close her hand around them.

"Whoa, Pebbles," she said. "Steady boy."

At last Pebbles slowed.

"Good pony, good boy," said Natty in her most soothing tones. "Good fella."

By the time they came to a stop, Pebbles was no longer showing the whites of his eyes and although blowing, seemed calmer.

"I don't blame you for being frightened by the splashes," soothed Natty, stroking his neck.

Ned turned and the ponies trotted back side by side along the path.

"No one's going to recognize me, are they?" she asked.

"They certainly are not," said Ned. "Trust your disguise, Natty. You'll be a stranger to them all."

She hoped Ned was right.

Nearing the bridge they were met by quite a sight. The water flowed at shoulder height and everyone in it was thoroughly soaked. Penelope was being pushed on to the bridge by Jamie and was shouting furious insults at Smudger. On the other side the skinny twins were trying unsuccessfully to help Smudger lift his bike from the water.

"I still don't see how we're going to get Jamie's helmet back," said Natty.

"You offer to pull out Smudger's bike in return for it," said Ned, keeping his voice low so as not to be heard by the others.

Once Penelope was out of the water, the skinny twins jumped to keep out of reach of her flailing riding crop. On the bank Henry was hopping from one foot to the other, uncertain of what to do, and Ben was holding his and Jamie's bikes ready to defend them against any threat.

To attract Penelope's attention Ned whinnied loudly.

"My pony," she cried when she saw them. "Pebbles!" She gave one last swipe and squelched across the bridge. When she reached Natty she took the offered reins. "He bolted," she said, as if Natty didn't know. "Lucky you were passing. That idiotic boy in the water frightened him. I'm soaked." She turned to Jamie who stood dripping behind her. "Thank you, Jamie, you're a hero," she said and swung herself into the saddle. "I'm going before I catch pneumonia."

And Penelope scowled one last time at Smudger before turning Pebbles and setting off for home in a very bad mood.

"Everyone all right?" Natty asked brightly when she was gone.

"Just a bit wet," said Jamie, with a shy smile. "Okay Smudger, give me back my bike helmet."

"Yes, give him back his bike helmet," said Natty. Everyone turned to look at her. Smudger's bike slipped back into the water for the umpteenth time and his teeth were heard to chatter. "And I'll get my pony to pull your bike out of the river."

"It's a deal," said the miserable Smudger.

"Helmet first," said Jamie, shooting a grateful look in Natty's direction. Smudger undid the chin strap and tossed it to Jamie. Jamie pulled it on and fastened it.

"Excuse me, but how did you know he'd stolen my helmet?" he asked.

"Oh, when our paths crossed earlier he wasn't wearing one," said Natty simply.

"Pass the rope then," said Jamie.

Rope! thought Natty and realized that

until this moment she hadn't given a thought to how she was going to do the pulling. She looked behind her to where a coil was fastened to the saddle. It hadn't been there earlier but she knew better than to question Ned's magic. He pawed the ground impatiently until she untied it and tossed one end to Jamie. She tied her end around Ned's neck.

Jamie threw the rope to Smudger and when it was fastened round the handlebars, Ned turned and pulled. The bike glided through the water to the bank. Henry and the skinny twins lifted it clear of a tree root and it was back on dry land. Jamie undid the knot while the twins took a hand each and hauled Smudger up the bank. He nodded in Natty's direction.

"Thanks."

"Not at all," said Natty, coiling the rope and tying it back to the saddle. Jamie took his bike from Ben.

"Yes, thanks very much," he said. Natty couldn't help a grin, thrilled that even her own brother hadn't recognized her in her magic riding clothes.

"Glad to have helped," she said, wondering how Jamie was going to explain his soaking clothes to Mum. "Goodbye."

Ned set off at a steady trot towards home and Jamie and Ben peddled after them, leaving the gang to see if their leader's bike was damaged.

"Hold tight," said Ned. "We'd better get a move on. We've got to get back before Jamie and Ben." He broke into an exhilarating gallop which ate up the ground, and he didn't slow until they came out of the wood on to the lane. When they reached Natty's front gate, the rushing wind spun them tiny again. They squeezed through the gap at the bottom of the gate and were across the grass in no time. Jumping up the fig-tree leaves was much less daunting than jumping down. Besides, Natty was feeling more confident after her ride.

They reached the window-sill just as Jamie and Ben coasted up to the side gate where they said a cheery goodbye to each other. Ned quickly stepped over the sill to the safety of Natty's bedroom.

"What an adventure," she said, dismounting and giving Ned a big hug. "Thank you for saving the day."

"We did it together." Ned tossed his head. "No need to go down the steps. Just let go of the reins and jump." Natty did so without thinking and leapt into a whirling wind. In a trice she was standing next to the Lego steps, her proper size again, once more in her sweatshirt, jeans and trainers. As for Ned, he was back in his picture.

Outside she heard the whirr of bicycle tyres on the lane. A dripping Smudger Evans, trailed by his forlorn gang, was pedalling for home.

"It really was a wonderful adventure, Ned," she said, wistfully running her finger across the glossy pony poster. "Jamie got his bike helmet back and not one of them guessed it was me."

Then she opened the door and hurried downstairs. From the living-room she could see Mum and Jamie on the grass. She darted into the kitchen and put her head round the back door.

"Can we make the cake now?" she asked and then, with an impish grin, said, "Oh, Jamie. You're all wet."

"Don't you start," Jamie said. "I fell in the river. Okay? But it was worth it."

"Some argument about his bike helmet," said Mum, shaking her head. "Now go on. Upstairs and get in the bath."

"Mum, don't fuss."

"I'm not. I don't want you getting a chill, that's all."

"Can I get the cake things out?" Natty asked. "And can it be a chocolate one?"

"If you like," said Mum. "I'll lock up the shed and we can start." Jamie sat on the step and pulled off his squelching trainers.

"Can it have chocolate icing?" he said.

"I'll ask Mum. I know there's a packet of chocolate buttons in the cupboard."

"Yum," said Jamie. "I'll help decorate it when I've had my bath. Oh, and I'll tell you how I beat Smudger Evans and his gang. Me, Ben, Penelope Potter and this mystery girl on a chestnut pony."

"Oh?"

"Yes, you'll never believe what happened. It was amazing."

And he padded into the living-room, leaving Natty to undo a packet of flour and smile a secret smile.

The End